little Miss Sunshine

by Roger Hargreaves

Welcome to Miseryland.

We say 'welcome', but there really isn't very much to welcome you about it.

It's the most miserable place in the world.

Miseryland worms look like this!

And when the birds wake up in the morning in Miseryland, they don't start singing.

They start crying!

Oh, it really is an awful place!

And the King of Miseryland is even worse.

He sits on his throne all day long with tears streaming down his face.

"Oh I'm so unhappy," he keeps sobbing, over and over and over again.

Dear, oh dear, oh dear!

Little Miss Sunshine had been on holiday.

She'd had a lovely time, and now she was driving home.

She was whistling happily to herself as she drove along when, out of the corner of her eye, she saw a signpost.

To Miseryland.

"Miseryland?" she thought to herself.

"I've never heard of that before!"

And she turned off down the road.

She came to a sign which read:

YOU ARE NOW ENTERING MISERYLAND

And underneath it said:

SMILING

LAUGHING

CHUCKLING

GIGGLING

FORBIDDEN

By Order of the King.

"Oh dear," thought little Miss Sunshine as she drove along.

She came to a castle with a huge door.

A soldier stopped her.

"What do you want?" he asked gloomily.

"I want to see the King," smiled little Miss Sunshine.

"You're under arrest," said the soldier.

"But why?" asked little Miss Sunshine.

"For a most serious crime," replied the soldier.

"Most serious indeed!"

The soldier marched little Miss Sunshine through the huge door.

And across a courtyard.

And through another huge door.

And up an enormous staircase.

And along a long corridor.

And through another huge door.

And into a gigantic room.

And at the end of the gigantic room sat the King.

Crying his eyes out!

"Your Majesty," said the soldier, bowing low, "I have arrested this person for a most serious crime!"

The King stopped crying.

"She smiled at me," said the soldier.

There was a shocked silence.

"She did WHAT?" cried the King.

"She smiled at me," repeated the soldier.

"But why is smiling not allowed?" laughed little Miss Sunshine.

"She LAUGHED at me," cried the King.

"Why not?" she chuckled.

"She CHUCKLED!" cried the King.

Little Miss Sunshine giggled.

"She GIGGLED!" went on the King.

And he burst into tears again.

"But why are these things not allowed?"
asked little Miss Sunshine.

"Because this is Miseryland," wept the King.

"And they've never been allowed," he sobbed.

"Oh, I was so unhappy before you arrived,"
he wailed, "but now I'm twice as unhappy!"

Little Miss Sunshine looked at him.

"But wouldn't you like to be happy?"
she asked.

"Of course I would," cried the King.

"But how can I be? This is MISERYLAND!"

Little Miss Sunshine thought.

"Come on," she said.

"You can't talk to me like that," sobbed the King.

"Don't be silly," she replied, and led him across the gigantic room, and through the huge door, and along the long corridor, and down the enormous staircase, and through the huge door, and across the courtyard, and through the huge door, to her car.

"Get in," she said.

Little Miss Sunshine drove the crying King
back to the large notice.

"Dry your eyes," she said, and handed him
a large handkerchief from her handbag.

And then, from her handbag, she produced
a large pen.

Five minutes later she'd finished.

Instead of saying:

YOU ARE NOW ENTERING MISERYLAND
    SMILING
    LAUGHING
    CHUCKLING
    GIGGLING
    FORBIDDEN
    By Order of the King.

Do you know what it said now?

YOU ARE NOW ENTERING LAUGHTERLAND
  SMILING
  LAUGHING
  CHUCKLING
  GIGGLING
  PERMITTED
  By Order of the King

"There," said little Miss Sunshine. "Now you can be happy."

"But I don't know HOW to be happy," sniffed the King.

"I've never TRIED it!"

"Nonsense," said little Miss Sunshine.

"It's really very easy," she smiled.

The King tried a smile.

"Not bad," she laughed.

The King tried a laugh.

"Getting better," she chuckled.

The king tried a chuckle.

"You've got it," she giggled.

The King looked at her.

"So I have," he giggled.

"I'm the King of Laughterland!"

As little Miss Sunshine arrived home, there was Mr Happy out for an evening stroll.

"Hello," he grinned. "Where have you been?"

"Miseryland!" she replied.

"Miseryland?" he said.

"I didn't know there was such a place!"

Little Miss Sunshine giggled.

"Actually," she said.

"There isn't!"

3 Great Offers for MR.MEN Fans!

MR.MEN TOKEN

1 New Mr. Men or Little Miss Library Bus Presentation Cases

A brand new stronger, roomier school bus library box, with sturdy carrying handle and stay-closed fasteners.

The full colour, wipe-clean boxes make a great home for your full collection.

They're just £5.99 inc P&P and free bookmark!

☐ MR. MEN   ☐ LITTLE MISS (please tick and order overleaf)

2 Door Hangers and Posters

In every Mr. Men and Little Miss book like this one, you will find a special token. Collect 6 tokens and we will send you a brilliant Mr. Men or Little Miss poster and a Mr. Men or Little Miss double sided full colour bedroom door hanger of your choice. Simply tick your choice in the list and tape a 50p coin for your two items to this page.

PLEASE STICK YOUR 50P COIN HERE

Door Hangers (please tick)
☐ Mr. Nosey & Mr. Muddle
☐ Mr. Slow & Mr. Busy
☐ Mr. Messy & Mr. Quiet
☐ Mr. Perfect & Mr. Forgetful
☐ Little Miss Fun & Little Miss Late
☐ Little Miss Helpful & Little Miss Tidy
☐ Little Miss Busy & Little Miss Brainy
☐ Little Miss Star & Little Miss Fun

Posters (please tick)
☐ MR.MEN
☐ LITTLE MISS

3 Sixteen Beautiful Fridge Magnets – any 2 for £2.00!
inc.P&P

They're very special collector's items!
Simply tick your first and second* choices from the list below
of any 2 characters!

1st Choice
- [ ] Mr. Happy
- [ ] Mr. Lazy
- [ ] Mr. Topsy-Turvy
- [ ] Mr. Bounce
- [ ] Mr. Bump
- [ ] Mr. Small
- [ ] Mr. Snow
- [ ] Mr. Wrong

- [ ] Mr. Daydream
- [ ] Mr. Tickle
- [ ] Mr. Greedy
- [ ] Mr. Funny
- [ ] Little Miss Giggles
- [ ] Little Miss Splendid
- [ ] Little Miss Naughty
- [ ] Little Miss Sunshine

2nd Choice
- [ ] Mr. Happy
- [ ] Mr. Lazy
- [ ] Mr. Topsy-Turvy
- [ ] Mr. Bounce
- [ ] Mr. Bump
- [ ] Mr. Small
- [ ] Mr. Snow
- [ ] Mr. Wrong

- [ ] Mr. Daydream
- [ ] Mr. Tickle
- [ ] Mr. Greedy
- [ ] Mr. Funny
- [ ] Little Miss Giggles
- [ ] Little Miss Splendid
- [ ] Little Miss Naughty
- [ ] Little Miss Sunshine

*Only in case your first choice is out of stock.

--- TO BE COMPLETED BY AN ADULT ---

**To apply for any of these great offers, ask an adult to complete the coupon below and send it with
the appropriate payment and tokens, if needed, to MR. MEN OFFERS, PO BOX 7, MANCHESTER M19 2HD**

- [ ] Please send _____ Mr. Men Library case(s) and/or _____ Little Miss Library case(s) at £5.99 each inc P&P
- [ ] Please send a poster and door hanger as selected overleaf. I enclose six tokens plus a 50p coin for P&P
- [ ] Please send me _____ pair(s) of Mr. Men/Little Miss fridge magnets, as selected above at £2.00 inc P&P

Fan's Name _____

Address _____

_____ **Postcode** _____

Date of Birth _____

Name of Parent/Guardian _____

Total amount enclosed £ _____

- [ ] **I enclose a cheque/postal order payable to Egmont Books Limited**
- [ ] **Please charge my MasterCard/Visa/Amex/Switch or Delta account** (delete as appropriate)

Card Number

Expiry date ___/___ **Signature** _____

Please allow 28 days for delivery. We reserve the right to change the terms of this offer at any time but we offer
a 14 day money back guarantee. This does not affect your statutory rights. Data Protection Act: If you do not wish
to receive other similar offers from us or companies we recommend, please tick this box [ ]. Offers apply to UK only.

MR.MEN   LITTLE MISS
Mr. Men and Little Miss™ ©Mrs. Roger Hargreaves

CUT ALONG DOTTED LINE AND RETURN THIS WHOLE PAGE